W9-CPE-979

ABOUT THE BANK STREET READY-TO-READ SERIES

More than seventy-five years of educational research, innovative teaching, and quality publishing have earned The Bank Street College of Education its reputation as America's most trusted name in early childhood education.

Because no two children are exactly alike in their development, the Bank Street Ready-to-Read series is written on three levels to accommodate the individual stages of reading readiness of children ages three through eight.

- *Level 1:* **GETTING READY TO READ** (Pre-K–Grade 1)
  Level 1 books are perfect for reading aloud with children who are getting ready to read or just starting to read words or phrases. These books feature large type, repetition, and simple sentences.

- *Level 2:* **READING TOGETHER** (Grades 1–3)
  These books have slightly smaller type and longer sentences. They are ideal for children beginning to read by themselves who may need help.

- *Level 3:* **I CAN READ IT MYSELF** (Grades 2–3)
  These stories are just right for children who can read independently. They offer more complex and challenging stories and sentences.

All three levels of The Bank Street Ready-to-Read books make it easy to select the books most appropriate for your child's development and enable him or her to grow with the series step by step. The levels purposely overlap to reinforce skills and further encourage reading.

We feel that making reading fun is the single most important thing anyone can do to help children become good readers. We hope you will become part of Bank Street's long tradition of learning through sharing.

The Bank Street College
of Education

E
K
c. 1

To Matthew
and the next generation
of chocolate lovers
—E.J.S.

CHOCO-LOUIE

A Bantam Book/March 1996

Published by Bantam Doubleday Dell Books
for Young Readers, a division of Bantam
Doubleday Dell Publishing Group, Inc.
1540 Broadway, New York, New York 10036.

Special thanks to Hope Innelli and Kathy Huck.

The trademarks "Bantam Books" and the
portrayal of a rooster are registered
in the U.S. Patent and Trademark Office
and in other countries. Marca Registrada.

Library of Congress Cataloging-in-Publication Data

Kindley, Jeffrey.
Choco-Louie / by Jeffrey Kindley;
illustrated by Ellen Joy Sasaki.
p.   cm.—(A Bank Street ready-to-read)
"A Byron Preiss book."
Summary: Louie's older brother bets his new skateboard
that Louie can't go for an entire week
without eating any chocolate.
ISBN 0-553-09744-X (hard cover).—ISBN 0-553-37576-8 (trade paper)
[1. Chocolate—Fiction.   2. Wagers—Fiction.   3. Brothers—Fiction.]
I. Sasaki, Ellen Joy, ill.   II. Title.   III. Series.
PZ7.K5668Ch   1996
[E]—dc20
94-49334   CIP   AC

Published simultaneously in the United States and Canada

PRINTED IN THE UNITED STATES OF AMERICA

0 9 8 7 6 5 4 3 2 1

Choco-Louie

by Jeff Kindley
Illustrated by Ellen Joy Sasaki

A Byron Preiss Book

BANTAM BOOKS
NEW YORK • TORONTO • LONDON • SYDNEY • AUCKLAND

Louie was crazy about chocolate.
"You love it way too much,"
said his big brother, Ben.
"You've turned into Choco-Louie."

4

Louie loved Fudgy Flippers,
the breakfast food
with little chocolate dolphins
in every bite.

He begged his dad to buy
Cocoa Loco Super-Sips
and Loony Loony Fudge-A-Roonies
and Choco-Wocko Tacos.

But best of all Louie loved
Double Dark Dunkos.
"They're super-delicious," he said,
"the yummiest cookies there are."

First Louie opened up his Dunko
and licked off the creamy part.
He loved the taste and the feel
of the chocolate cream on his tongue.

Slowly he lowered
the crunchy cookie into his milk.
Then he waited till it was
mooshy enough to slurp.

"Yum yummy," said Louie.
"Yum yummy.
Yum yummy, yum yummy,
yum yum."

Louie opened up another Dunko
and stuck out his tongue to lick it.
"You are making me sick," said Ben.
"You don't have to watch," said Louie.

"You couldn't live without chocolate, could you?" asked Ben.
"Sure I could," said Louie.
"But I wouldn't want to."

"I bet you couldn't," said Ben.
"You're Choco-Louie.
I bet anything you couldn't live
without chocolate for one whole week."

"Anything?" asked Louie.
He stopped dunking and looked at Ben.
"You bet anything?
Even your new skateboard?"

"Why not?" said Ben.
"No way you could last seven whole days."
"That's what *you* think," said Louie.
He dumped his Dunkos in the trash.

Monday was easy for Louie.
He ate Smart Bran for breakfast.
On Tuesday he didn't trade his yogurt
for Anna's chocolate pudding at lunch.

On Wednesday he went
to Franco's birthday party.
Ben peeked through the window
to watch what Louie ate.

17

The birthday cake was a mountain
of yummy fudge.
Franco's mom held out a piece.
"No, thank you," Louie said sadly.

Louie sat watching the others eat.
"Yum yummy," said Ben
as he gobbled up Louie's cake.
"Yum yummy, yum yummy, yum yum."

19

On Thursday Great-aunt Irene
came to visit.
She brought a special treat:
homemade chocolate-chip cookies.

20

"I'm not really hungry," said Louie.
"I hope you're not getting sick,"
said Louie's mom.
"Oh wow, are they yummy!" said Ben.

On Friday Louie didn't trade
his apple juice for Josh's chocolate milk.
Emily said he could have her brownie
for his fig bars, but he said no.

On Saturday Louie's soccer coach
asked the team to sell
Fudgie-Wudgies to raise money.
Louie's eyes got all wet and blinky.

Then came Sunday,
the very last day of the bet.
Louie woke up to find a glass of milk
and a pile of Dunkos beside his bed.

"Go ahead, enjoy yourself," said Ben.
"You deserve it, old buddy, old pal."
"You're right," said Choco-Louie.
"I *do* deserve it."

He opened up a Double Dark Dunko.
He stuck out his tongue to lick it,
but then he stopped.
"What are you waiting for?" asked Ben.

26

"I'm thinking how much better
this will taste tomorrow," said Louie.
"*After* I ride my brand-new skateboard."
"Oh no!" wailed Ben. "I was so close!"

On Monday Louie went sailing
down the street on his new skateboard.
"Hey, look at me!" he yelled to Ben.
"I'm Skateboard Louie!"

But then he hit a bump and fell off.
"Ouch!" said Louie. "That hurt!"
"Want me to teach you how to ride?"
asked Ben.

Ben taught Louie his skateboard tricks
all afternoon.
He taught him his twists and flips
and special glide.

Then it was time for a snack.
Louie opened his bag of Dunkos.
"I bet you'll really enjoy
those now," said Ben.

"I bet we both will," said Louie.
And they did.